ELISABETH

C L A I R E   A .   N I V O L A

F R A N C E S   F O S T E R   B O O K S

F A R R A R   S T R A U S   G I R O U X

N E W   Y O R K

*This is my mother's story.
She wanted it told for all
the children of the world
who have had to leave what
they love behind.*

A long time ago, when I was a little girl in
Germany, I had a doll named Elisabeth. We loved
each other so dearly that we shared everything.

We slept in the same bed and ate from a single dish. The sun shone down on both of us, and together we cast one shadow.

We had many friends in common. There was the dainty frog, found in a nearby pond, who foretold the weather. He climbed his wooden ladder when the day was to be sunny and plunged back down when it was going to rain.

There was the turtle, brought from Africa by an eccentric
uncle, who took us for rides on its great plated back.

It had the slow, sure steps of one who had lived a long time, and who—I liked to believe—would live forever.

And there was my dog, Fifi, mischievous and impatient, who liked Elisabeth so much that he once asked her to dance. When she would not answer his high-pitched barks . . .

Fifi bit into Elisabeth's arm to get a good grip on her

and then dragged her dancing about the room.

Poor, poor Elisabeth! What would she have done had I not saved her! I rushed downstairs to my father, who was a doctor and had his office in our house. Together we bound up the wound.

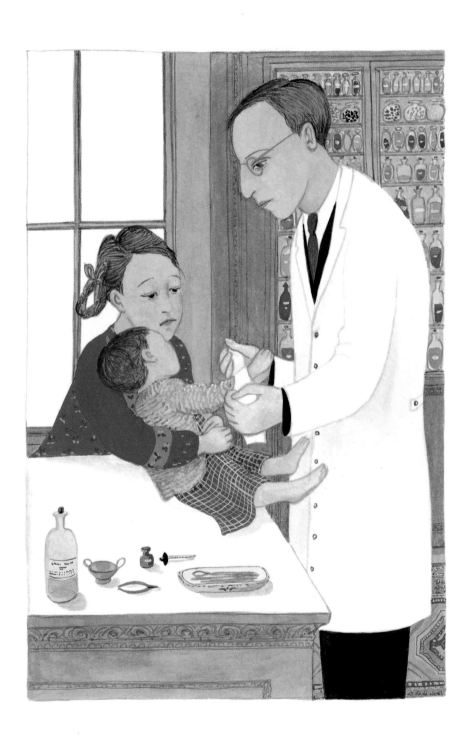

Then everything changed. In school, the teacher no longer saw my hand when I raised it in class. "Jew," I was called.

A soldier patrolled our front door, making sure that only Jewish patients entered to see my father.

One morning, my parents woke me while it was still
dark. I heard fear in their voices: "Quickly! We must go!"
The fear took hold inside me. "Carry nothing," they
warned. "We must not arouse suspicion." I did not fully
understand. We left everything behind.

Everything—even Elisabeth. "I will come back for you,"
I had whispered to her and all that was in my room, as
my mother tugged at me to hurry. Later, when I thought
of Elisabeth, I wept for both of us. It was hard for me,
but what would become of Elisabeth without me?

We fled first to Italy and from there to Paris and on to America. We never went back. The years passed. I grew up, married, and had a family.

We settled near the seashore in a town far across the ocean from the continent where I had lived as a child with Elisabeth.

When my daughter was almost six, she asked for only one thing for her birthday. She wanted a doll that would fill her arms like a real baby.

I went from shop to shop. Because of Elisabeth, no doll could please me. Then one day, as I was passing an

antique store, my eye was caught by a doll in the cluttered window. I stepped inside.

How I liked her! Her smell reminded me of my childhood. "She'll be much too expensive in a shop like this," I told myself, holding her small hand in mine. Her lace sleeve fell back, and it was then that I saw the two teeth marks—exactly where Fifi had bitten Elisabeth so many years ago!

"You mustn't touch the objects," said the stern shopkeeper. But already I had her in my arms. I was going to buy her and take her home to my daughter.

Again, many years have passed. My daughter has grown up, and now her little girl takes care of Elisabeth. She, too, knows this story well. Sometimes we wonder together—as I'm sure you will—how Elisabeth came to find me and mend my heart after so many years and across such a wide ocean.

Published in Canada by HarperCollins*CanadaLtd*

Color separations by Hong Kong Scanner Arts

Printed and bound in the United States of America by Berryville Graphics

Typography by Filomena Tuosto

First edition, 1997

Second printing, 1997

Library of Congress Cataloging-in-Publication Data

Nivola, Claire A.

    Elisabeth / Claire Nivola. — 1st ed.

      p.   cm.

    "Frances Foster books."

    Summary: Forced to flee the Nazis, a young girl and her family eventually end up in the United States where, years later, with a young daughter of her own, she is improbably reunited with the beloved doll she left behind in Germany.

    ISBN 0-374-32085-3

    [1. Dolls—Fiction. 2. Jews—Germany—Fiction.] I. Title.

PZ7.N6435E1   1997

[E]—dc20   96-23877